30

Little Monster Did It!

Helen Cooper

DOUBLEDAY

LONDON · NEW YORK · TORONTO · SYDNEY · AUCKLAND

For Anik

TRANSWORLD PUBLISHERS LTD
61-63 Uxbridge Road, London W5 5SA
TRANSWORLD PUBLISHERS (AUSTRALIA) PTY LTD
15-25 Helles Avenue, Moorebank, NSW 2170
TRANSWORLD PUBLISHERS (NZ) LTD
3 William Pickering Drive, Albany, Auckland

DOUBLEDAY CANADA LTD
105 Bond Street, Toronto, Ontario M5B lY3
Published l995 by Doubleday
a division of Transworld Publishers Ltd

ISBN 0 385 406207

Printed in Belgium

I liked it best with just us three,
only Mum and Dad and me,
and it was quiet in our house…

…most of the time.

Then before Mum went to hospital,
she gave a present to me.

It had a label on it.
The label said:

Dear Amy,
this little monster
wants to be your
friend
xx

And he did! He loved me…

But he didn't love the new baby.

Mum came in all happy.
'Come and see your little brother,' she smiled.
'Isn't he sweet?'

'I think he's very nice,' I said,
'but Little Monster hates him!'

Later we helped Dad.

But Little Monster had
a little accident...

...and the nappies smelt really, really bad.   So we left.

'Come and have a quiet cuddle,' said Mum.

But Little Monster couldn't keep still,
and the baby wouldn't feed,
and there wasn't much room for me.

So we went upstairs where we
could stomp like elephants.

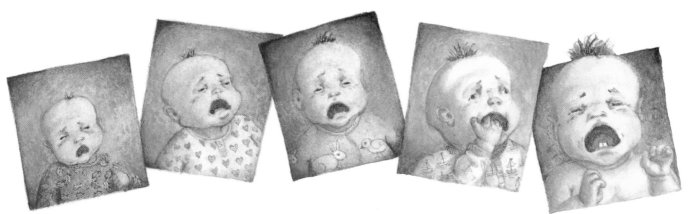

Every night for weeks and weeks,
the baby wouldn't go to sleep.

The noise went on all winter,
and it gave Little Monster bad dreams.

Then we'd both be awake, so...

...we'd visit Mum.

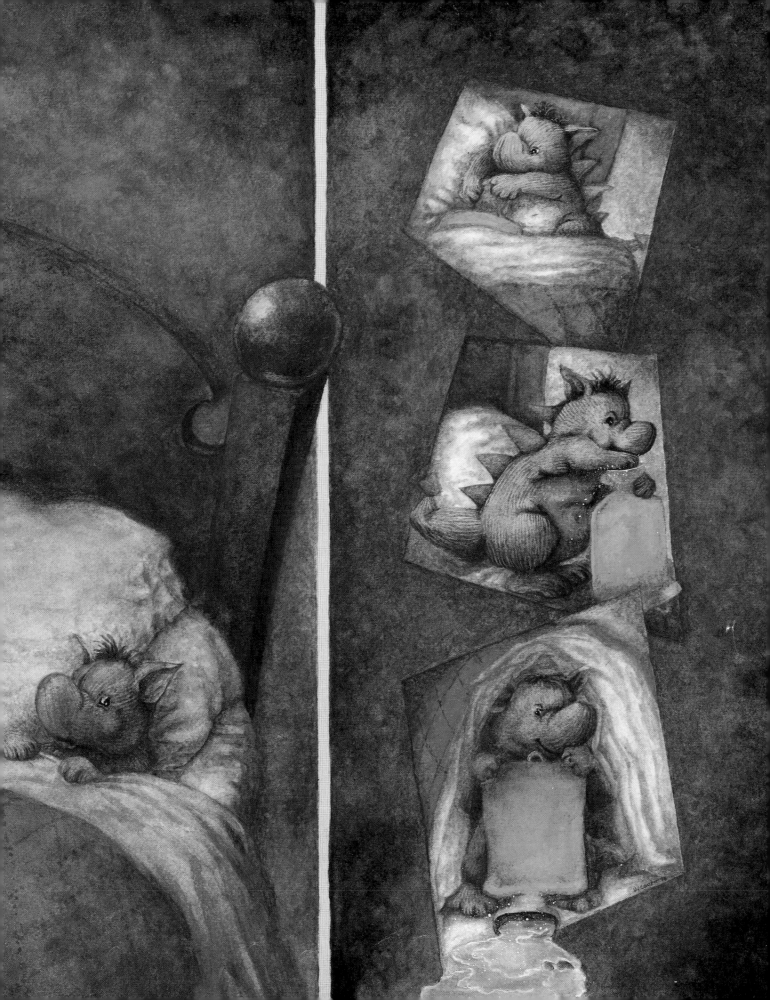

One night the bed got really wet.
'But Little Monster did it!' I said…

And he had.
He'd emptied the hot water bottle.

'Back to your room,' yelled Dad,
'until you can be good!'

But Little Monster
didn't want to be good there either.

The next day was even worse.

The video broke.

Little Monster did it.

The floor was soaked.

Little Monster did it.

The baby woke.

Little Monster did it.

'If this goes on,
he'll have to go!' yelled Dad.

'No!' I shouted, and we ran upstairs.

Mum called us to see if we could all be friends.
But Little Monster wouldn't.

'Can't we send the baby back?' I asked.
Mum said we couldn't.
'He needs us to look after him,' she said.
'What would he do on his own?'

'What would he do on his own?'
I thought about it…

Then I helped him
dry his toes.

And I told him stories until he went to sleep.

Little Monster wasn't pleased –
he dragged me off to bed.

The next
morning
Little Monster
woke up
very early.
When I went
downstairs
with Mum
and Dad
we saw…

…a huge heap
on the kitchen floor!
Little Monster had
been doing some
spring-cleaning!

'Little Monster
has to go,'

yelled Mum.

'Right now!'

Where could we hide?

There was only one safe place!

Mum and Dad came puffing upstairs.

They looked at me and my baby brother.

They looked at Little Monster.

They looked at each other…

...and they smiled.

Then we went away, just us three,
to make some tea and some juice for me.
Dad said Little Monster could stay.
I said my brother could too.
'We'll have some peace and quiet now,
won't we!' smiled Mum.

Maybe we will…

I'll have to ask Little Monster.

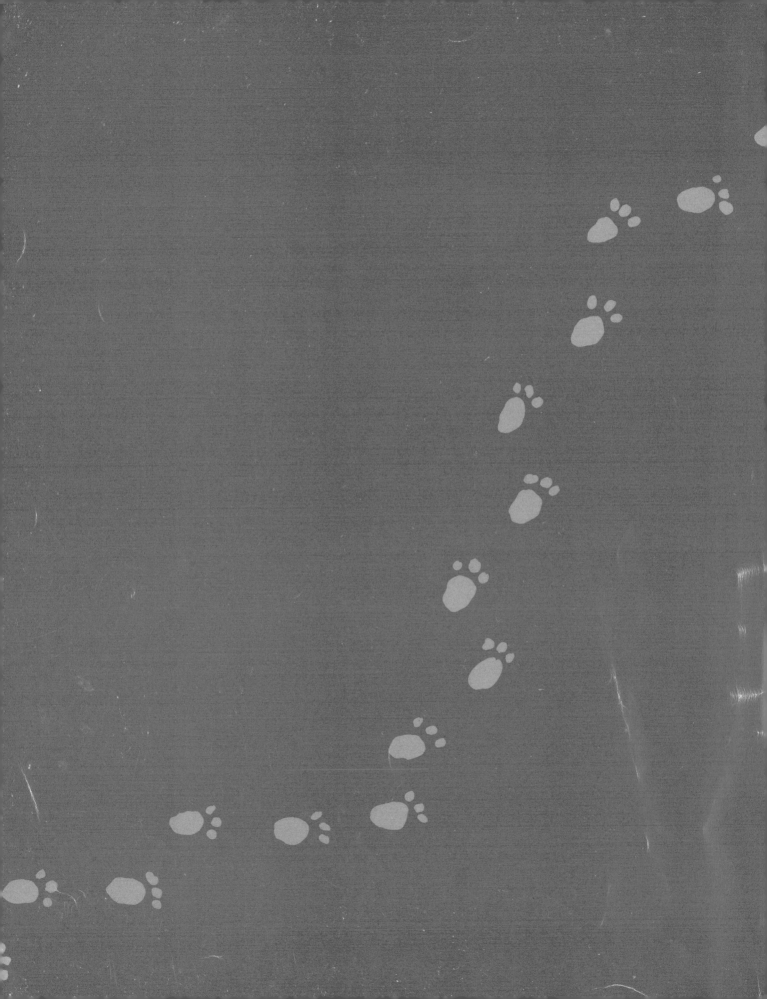